KATE CHOPIN

THE KISS
AND OTHER STORIES

PENGUIN BOOKS

PENGUIN BOOKS

Published by the Penguin Group
Penguin Books Ltd, 27 Wrights Lane, London w8 5TZ, England
Penguin Books USA Inc., 375 Hudson Street, New York, New York 10014, USA
Penguin Books Australia Ltd, Ringwood, Victoria, Australia
Penguin Books Canada Ltd, 10 Alcorn Avenue, Toronto, Ontario, Canada M4V 3B2
Penguin Books (NZ) Ltd, 182–190 Wairau Road, Auckland 10, New Zealand

Penguin Books Ltd, Registered Offices: Harmondsworth, Middlesex, England

These stories are from *A Vocation and a Voice*, edited by Emily Toth,
and *The Awakening and Selected Stories*, edited by Sandra M. Gilbert,
published in Penguin Classics 1991 and 1986
This edition published 1995
1 3 5 7 9 10 8 6 4 2

Printed in England by Clays Ltd, St Ives plc

CONTENTS

The Kiss   1

Désirée's Baby   6

The Story of an Hour   15

The Unexpected   20

The Godmother   26

The Kiss

It was still quite light out of doors, but inside with the curtains drawn and the smouldering fire sending out a dim, uncertain glow, the room was full of deep shadows.

Brantain sat in one of these shadows; it had overtaken him and he did not mind. The obscurity lent him courage to keep his eyes fastened as ardently as he liked upon the girl who sat in the firelight.

She was very handsome, with a certain fine, rich coloring that belongs to the healthy brune type. She was quite composed, as she idly stroked the satiny coat of the cat that lay curled in her lap, and she occasionally sent a slow glance into the shadow where her companion sat. They were talking low, of indifferent things which plainly were not the things that occupied their thoughts. She knew that he loved her—a frank, blustering fellow without guile enough to conceal his feelings, and no desire to do so. For two weeks past he had sought her society eagerly and persistently. She was confidently waiting for him to declare himself and she meant to accept him. The rather insignificant and unattractive Brantain was enormously rich; and she liked and required the entourage which wealth could give her.

During one of the pauses between their talk of the last tea and the next reception the door opened and a young man entered whom Brantain knew quite well. The girl turned her face toward him. A stride or two brought him to her side, and bending over her chair—before she could suspect his intention, for she did not realize that he had not seen her visitor—he pressed an ardent, lingering kiss upon her lips.

Brantain slowly arose; so did the girl arise, but quickly, and the newcomer stood between them, a little amusement and some defiance struggling with the confusion in his face.

"I believe," stammered Brantain, "I see that I have stayed too long. I—I had no idea—that is, I must wish you good-bye." He was clutching his hat with both hands, and probably did not perceive that she was extending her hand to him, her presence of mind had not completely deserted her; but she could not have trusted herself to speak.

"Hang me if I saw him sitting there, Nattie! I know it's deuced awkward for you. But I hope you'll forgive me this once—this very first break. Why, what's the matter?"

"Don't touch me; don't come near me," she returned angrily. "What do you mean by entering the house without ringing?"

"I came in with your brother, as I often do," he answered coldly, in self-justification. "We came in the side way. He went upstairs and I came in here hoping to find you. The explanation is simple enough and ought to satisfy you that the misadventure was unavoidable. But do say that you forgive me, Nathalie," he entreated, softening.

"Forgive you! You don't know what you are talking about. Let me pass. It depends upon—a good deal whether I ever forgive you."

At that next reception which she and Brantain had been talking about she approached the young man with a delicious frankness of manner when she saw him there.

"Will you let me speak to you a moment or two, Mr. Brantain?" she asked with an engaging but perturbed smile. He seemed extremely unhappy; but when she took his arm and walked away with him, seeking a retired corner, a ray of hope mingled with the almost comical misery of his expression. She was apparently very outspoken.

"Perhaps I should not have sought this interview, Mr. Brantain; but—but, oh, I have been very uncomfortable, almost miserable since that little encounter the other afternoon. When I thought how you might have misinterpreted it, and believed things"—hope was plainly gaining the ascendancy over misery in Brantain's round, guileless face—"of course, I know it is nothing to you, but for my own sake I do want you to understand that Mr. Harvy is an intimate friend of long standing. Why, we have always been like cousins—like brother and sister, I may say. He is my brother's most intimate associate and often fancies that he is entitled to the same privileges as the family. Oh,

I know it is absurd, uncalled for, to tell you this; undignified even," she was almost weeping, "but it makes so much difference to me what you think of—of me." Her voice had grown very low and agitated. The misery had all disappeared from Brantain's face.

"Then you do really care what I think, Miss Nathalie? May I call you Miss Nathalie?" They turned into a long, dim corridor that was lined on either side with tall, graceful plants. They walked slowly to the very end of it. When they turned to retrace their steps Brantain's face was radiant and hers was triumphant.

Harvy was among the guests at the wedding; and he sought her out in a rare moment when she stood alone.

"Your husband," he said, smiling, "has sent me over to kiss you."

A quick blush suffused her face and round polished throat. "I suppose it's natural for a man to feel and act generously on an occasion of this kind. He tells me he doesn't want his marriage to interrupt wholly that pleasant intimacy which has existed between you and me. I don't know what you've been telling him," with an insolent smile, "but he has sent me here to kiss you."

She felt like a chess player who, by the clever handling of his pieces, sees the game taking the course intended. Her eyes were bright and tender with a smile as they glanced up into his; and her lips looked hungry for the kiss which they invited.

"But, you know," he went on quietly, "I didn't tell him so, it would have seemed ungrateful, but I can tell you. I've stopped kissing women; it's dangerous."

Well, she had Brantain and his million left. A person can't have everything in this world; and it was a little unreasonable of her to expect it.

Désirée's Baby

As the day was pleasant, Madame Valmondé drove over to L'Abri to see Désirée and the baby.

It made her laugh to think of Désirée with a baby. Why, it seemed but yesterday that Désirée was little more than a baby herself; when Monsieur in riding through the gateway of Valmondé had found her lying asleep in the shadow of the big stone pillar.

The little one awoke in his arms and began to cry for "Dada." That was as much as she could do or say. Some people thought she might have strayed there of her own accord, for she was of the toddling age. The prevailing belief was that she had been purposely left by a party of Texans, whose canvas-covered wagon, late in the day, had crossed the ferry that Coton Maïs kept, just below the plantation. In time Madame Valmondé abandoned every speculation but the one that Désirée had been sent to her by a beneficent Providence to be the child of her affection, seeing that she was without child of the flesh. For the girl grew to be beautiful and gentle, affectionate and sincere,—the idol of Valmondé.

It was no wonder, when she stood one day against the stone pillar in whose shadow she had lain asleep, eighteen years before, that Armand Aubigny riding by and seeing her there, had fallen in love with her. That was the way all the Aubignys fell in love, as if struck by a pistol shot. The wonder was that he had not loved her before; for he had known her since his father brought him home from Paris, a boy of eight, after his mother died there. The passion that awoke in him that day, when he saw her at the gate, swept along like an avalanche, or like a prairie fire, or like anything that drives headlong over all obstacles.

Monsieur Valmondé grew practical and wanted things well considered: that is, the girl's obscure origin. Armand looked into her eyes and did not care. He was reminded that she was nameless. What did it matter about a name when he could give her one of the oldest and proudest in Louisiana? He ordered the *corbeille* from Paris, and contained himself with what patience he could until it arrived; then they were married.

Madame Valmondé had not seen Désirée and the baby for four weeks. When she reached L'Abri she shuddered at the first sight of it, as she always did. It was a sad looking place, which for many years had not known the gentle presence of a mistress, old Monsieur Aubigny having married and buried his wife in France, and she having loved her own land too well ever to leave it. The roof came down steep and black like a cowl, reaching out beyond the wide galleries that encircled the yellow stuccoed house. Big, solemn oaks grew close to it, and their thick-leaved, far-reaching branches shadowed it like a pall.

Young Aubigny's rule was a strict one, too, and under i
his negroes had forgotten how to be gay, as they had beer
during the old master's easy-going and indulgent lifetime

The young mother was recovering slowly, and lay ful
length, in her soft white muslins and laces, upon a couch
The baby was beside her, upon her arm, where he had
fallen asleep, at her breast. The yellow nurse woman sa
beside a window fanning herself.

Madame Valmondé bent her portly figure over Désiré
and kissed her, holding her an instant tenderly in he
arms. Then she turned to the child.

"This is not the baby!" she exclaimed, in startled tones
French was the language spoken at Valmondé in thos
days.

"I knew you would be astonished," laughed Désirée
"at the way he has grown. The little *cocbon de lait!* Look
at his legs, mamma, and his hands and fingernails,—rea
finger-nails. Zandrine had to cut them this morning. Is n'
it true, Zandrine?"

The woman bowed her turbaned head majestically
"Mais si, Madame."

"And the way he cries," went on Désirée, "is deafening
Armand heard him the other day as far away as La
Blanche's cabin."

Madame Valmondé had never removed her eyes from
the child. She lifted it and walked with it over to the win
dow that was lightest. She scanned the baby narrowly

then looked as searchingly at Zandrine, whose face was turned to gaze across the fields.

"Yes, the child has grown, has changed," said Madame Valmondé, slowly, as she replaced it beside its mother. "What does Armand say?"

Désirée's face became suffused with a glow that was happiness itself.

"Oh, Armand is the proudest father in the parish, I believe, chiefly because it is a boy, to bear his name; though he says not,—that he would have loved a girl as well. But I know it is n't true. I know he says that to please me. And mamma," she added, drawing Madame Valmondé's head down to her and speaking in a whisper, "he has n't punished one of them—not one of them—since baby is born. Even Négrillon, who pretended to have burnt his leg that he might rest from work—he only laughed, and said Négrillon was a great scamp. Oh, mamma, I 'm so happy; it frightens me."

What Désirée said was true. Marriage, and later the birth of his son had softened Armand Aubigny's imperious and exacting nature greatly. This was what made the gentle Désirée so happy, for she loved him desperately. When he frowned she trembled, but loved him. When he smiled, she asked no greater blessing of God. But Armand's dark, handsome face had not often been disfigured by frowns since the day he fell in love with her.

When the baby was about three months old, Désirée awoke one day to the conviction that there was something in the air menacing her peace. It was at first too subtle to grasp. It had only been a disquieting suggestion; an air of mystery among the blacks; unexpected visits from far-off neighbors who could hardly account for their coming. Then a strange, an awful change in her husband's manner, which she dared not ask him to explain. When he spoke to her, it was with averted eyes, from which the old love-light seemed to have gone out. He absented himself from home; and when there, avoided her presence and that of her child, without excuse. And the very spirit of Satan seemed suddenly to take hold of him in his dealings with the slaves. Désirée was miserable enough to die.

She sat in her room, one hot afternoon, in her *peignoir*, listlessly drawing through her fingers the strands of her long, silky brown hair that hung about her shoulders. The baby, half naked, lay asleep upon her own great mahogany bed, that was like a sumptuous throne, with its satin-lined half-canopy. One of La Blanche's little quadroon boys—half naked too—stood fanning the child slowly with a fan of peacock feathers. Désirée's eyes had been fixed absently and sadly upon the baby, while she was striving to penetrate the threatening mist that she felt closing about her. She looked from her child to the boy who stood beside him, and back again, over and over. "Ah!" It was a cry that she could not help; which she was not conscious of having uttered. The blood turned like ice in her veins, and a clammy moisture gathered upon her face.

She tried to speak to the little quadroon boy; but no

sound would come, at first. When he heard his name uttered, he looked up, and his mistress was pointing to the door. He laid aside the great, soft fan, and obediently stole away, over the polished floor, on his bare tiptoes.

She stayed motionless, with gaze riveted upon her child, and her face the picture of fright.

Presently her husband entered the room, and without noticing her, went to a table and began to search among some papers which covered it.

"Armand," she called to him, in a voice which must have stabbed him, if he was human. But he did not notice. "Armand," she said again. Then she rose and tottered towards him. "Armand," she panted once more, clutching his arm, "look at our child. What does it mean? tell me."

He coldly but gently loosened her fingers from about his arm and thrust the hand away from him. "Tell me what it means!" she cried despairingly.

"It means," he answered lightly, "that the child is not white; it means that you are not white."

A quick conception of all that this accusation meant for her nerved her with unwonted courage to deny it. "It is a lie; it is not true, I am white! Look at my hair, it is brown; and my eyes are gray, Armand, you know they are gray. And my skin is fair," seizing his wrist. "Look at my hand; whiter than yours, Armand," she laughed hysterically.

"As white as La Blanche's," he returned cruelly; and went away leaving her alone with their child.

When she could hold a pen in her hand, she sent a despairing letter to Madame Valmondé.

"My mother, they tell me I am not white. Armand has told me I am not white. For God's sake tell them it is not true. You must know it is not true. I shall die. I must die. I cannot be so unhappy, and live."

The answer that came was as brief:

"My own Désirée: Come home to Valmondé; back to your mother who loves you. Come with your child."

When the letter reached Désirée she went with it to her husband's study, and laid it open upon the desk before which he sat. She was like a stone image; silent, white, motionless after she placed it there.

In silence he ran his cold eyes over the written words. He said nothing. "Shall I go, Armand?" she asked in tones sharp with agonized suspense.

"Yes, go."

"Do you want me to go?"

"Yes, I want you to go."

He thought Almighty God had dealt cruelly and unjustly with him; and felt, somehow, that he was paying Him back in kind when he stabbed thus into his wife's soul. Moreover he no longer loved her, because of the unconscious injury she had brought upon his home and his name.

She turned away like one stunned by a blow, and walked slowly towards the door, hoping he would call her back.

"Good-by, Armand," she moaned.

He did not answer her. That was his last blow at fate.

Désirée went in search of her child. Zandrine was pacing the sombre gallery with it. She took the little one from the nurse's arms with no word of explanation, and descending the steps, walked away, under the live-oak branches.

It was an October afternoon; the sun was just sinking. Out in the still fields the negroes were picking cotton.

Désirée had not changed the thin white garment nor the slippers which she wore. Her hair was uncovered and the sun's rays brought a golden gleam from its brown meshes. She did not take the broad, beaten road which led to the far-off plantation of Valmondé. She walked across a deserted field, where the stubble bruised her tender feet, so delicately shod, and tore her thin gown to shreds.

She disappeared among the reeds and willows that grew thick along the banks of the deep, sluggish bayou; and she did not come back again.

Some weeks later there was a curious scene enacted at L'Abri. In the centre of the smoothly swept back yard was a great bonfire. Armand Aubigny sat in the wide hallway that commanded a view of the spectacle; and it was he who dealt out to a half dozen negroes the material which kept this fire ablaze.

A graceful cradle of willow, with all its dainty furbishings, was laid upon the pyre, which had already been fed with the richness of a priceless *layette*. Then there were silk gowns, and velvet and satin ones added to these; laces, too, and embroideries; bonnets and gloves; for the *corbeille* had been of rare quality.

The last thing to go was a tiny bundle of letters; innocent little scribblings that Désirée had sent to him during the days of their espousal. There was the remnant of one back in the drawer from which he took them. But it was not Désirée's; it was part of an old letter from his mother to his father. He read it. She was thanking God for the blessing of her husband's love:—

"But, above all," she wrote, "night and day, I thank the good God for having so arranged our lives that our dear Armand will never know that his mother, who adores him, belongs to the race that is cursed with the brand of slavery."

The Story of an Hour
(The Dream of an Hour)

Knowing that Mrs. Mallard was afflicted with a heart trouble, great care was taken to break to her as gently as possible the news of her husband's death.

It was her sister Josephine who told her, in broken sentences; veiled hints that revealed in half concealing. Her husband's friend Richards was there, too, near her. It was he who had been in the newspaper office when intelligence of the railroad disaster was received, with Brently Mallard's name leading the list of "killed." He had only taken the time to assure himself of its truth by a second telegram, and had hastened to forestall any less careful, less tender friend in bearing the sad message.

She did not hear the story as many women have heard the same, with a paralyzed inability to accept its significance. She wept at once, with sudden, wild abandonment, in her sister's arms. When the storm of grief had spent itself she went away to her room alone. She would have no one follow her.

There stood, facing the open window, a comfortable, roomy armchair. Into this she sank, pressed down by a physical exhaustion that haunted her body and seemed to reach into her soul.

She could see in the open square before her house the tops of trees that were all aquiver with the new spring life. The delicious breath of rain was in the air. In the street below a peddler was crying his wares. The notes of a distant song which some one was singing reached her faintly, and countless sparrows were twittering in the eaves.

There were patches of blue sky showing here and there through the clouds that had met and piled one above the other in the west facing her window.

She sat with her head thrown back upon the cushion of the chair, quite motionless, except when a sob came up into her throat and shook her, as a child who has cried itself to sleep continues to sob in its dreams.

She was young, with a fair, calm face, whose lines bespoke repression and even a certain strength. But now there was a dull stare in her eyes, whose gaze was fixed away off yonder on one of those patches of blue sky. It was not a glance of reflection, but rather indicated a suspension of intelligent thought.

There was something coming to her and she was waiting for it, fearfully. What was it? She did not know; it was too subtle and elusive to name. But she felt it, creeping out of the sky, reaching toward her through the sounds, the scents, the color that filled the air.

Now her bosom rose and fell tumultuously. She was beginning to recognize this thing that was approaching to possess her, and she was striving to beat it back with her will—as powerless as her two white slender hands would have been.

When she abandoned herself a little whispered word escaped her slightly parted lips. She said it over and over under her breath: "free, free, free!" The vacant stare and the look of terror that had followed it went from her eyes. They stayed keen and bright. Her pulses beat fast, and the coursing blood warmed and relaxed every inch of her body.

She did not stop to ask if it were or were not a monstrous joy that held her. A clear and exalted perception enabled her to dismiss the suggestion as trivial.

She knew that she would weep again when she saw the kind, tender hands folded in death; the face that had never looked save with love upon her, fixed and gray and dead. But she saw beyond that bitter moment a long procession of years to come that would belong to her absolutely. And she opened and spread her arms out to them in welcome.

There would be no one to live for her during those coming years; she would live for herself. There would be no powerful will bending hers in that blind persistence with which men and women believe they have a right to impose a private will upon a fellow-creature. A kind intention or a cruel intention made the act seem no less a crime as she looked upon it in that brief moment of illumination.

And yet she had loved him—sometimes. Often she had not. What did it matter! What could love, the unsolved mystery, count for in face of this possession of self-assertion which she suddenly recognized as the strongest impulse of her being!

"Free! Body and soul free!" she kept whispering.

Josephine was kneeling before the closed door with her lips to the keyhole, imploring for admission. "Louise, open the door! I beg; open the door—you will make yourself ill. What are you doing, Louise? For heaven's sake open the door."

"Go away. I am not making myself ill." No; she was drinking in a very elixir of life through that open window.

Her fancy was running riot along those days ahead of her. Spring days, and summer days, and all sorts of days that would be her own. She breathed a quick prayer that life might be long. It was only yesterday she had thought with a shudder that life might be long.

She arose at length and opened the door to her sister's importunities. There was a feverish triumph in her eyes, and she carried herself unwittingly like a goddess of Victory. She clasped her sister's waist, and together they descended the stairs. Richards stood waiting for them at the bottom.

Some one was opening the front door with a latchkey. It was Brently Mallard who entered, a little travel-stained, composedly carrying his grip-sack and umbrella. He had been far from the scene of accident, and did not even know there had been one. He stood amazed at Josephine's piercing cry; at Richards' quick motion to screen him from the view of his wife.

But Richards was too late.

When the doctors came they said she had died of heart disease—of joy that kills.

The Unexpected

When Randall, for a brief absence, left his Dorothea, whom he was to marry after a time, the parting was bitter; the enforced separation seemed to them too cruel an ordeal to bear. The good-bye dragged with lingering kisses and sighs, and more kisses and more clinging till the last wrench came.

He was to return at the close of the month. Daily letters, impassioned and interminable, passed between them.

He did not return at the close of the month; he was delayed by illness. A heavy cold, accompanied by fever, contracted in some unaccountable way, held him to his bed. He hoped it would be over and that he would rejoin her in a week. But this was a stubborn cold, that seemed not to yield to familiar treatment; yet the physician was not discouraged, and promised to have him on his feet in a fortnight.

All this was torture to the impatient Dorothea; and if her parents had permitted, she surely would have hastened to the bedside of her beloved.

For a long interval he could not write himself. One day he seemed better; another day a "fresh cold" seized him ith relentless clutch; and so a second month went by, nd Dorothea had reached the limit of her endurance.

Then a tremulous scrawl came from him, saying he vould be obliged to pass a season at the south; but he vould first revisit his home, if only for a day, to clasp his earest one to his heart, to appease the hunger for her resence, the craving for her lips that had been devouring im through all the fever and pain of this detestable illess.

Dorothea had read his impassioned letters almost to atters. She had sat daily gazing for hours upon his porait, which showed him to be an almost perfect specimen f youthful health, strength and manly beauty.

She knew he would be altered in appearance—he had repared her, and had even written that she would hardly now him. She expected to see him ill and wasted; she vould not seem shocked; she would not let him see asonishment or pain in her face. She was in a quiver of nticipation, a sensuous fever of expectancy till he came.

She sat beside him on the sofa, for after the first delirus embrace he had been unable to hold himself upon his ottering feet, and had sunk exhausted in a corner of the ofa. He threw his head back upon the cushions and tayed, with closed eyes, panting; all the strength of his ody had concentrated in the clasp—the grasp with which e clung to her hand.

She stared at him as one might look upon a curious aparition which inspired wonder and mistrust rather than fear. This was not the man who had gone away from her the man she loved and had promised to marry. What hideous transformation had he undergone, or what devilish transformation was she undergoing in contemplating him? His skin was waxy and hectic, red upon the cheek-bones. His eyes were sunken; his features pinched and prominent; and his clothing hung loosely upon his wasted frame. The lips with which he had kissed her so hungrily and with which he was kissing her now, were dry and parched, and his breath was feverish and tainted.

At the sight and the touch of him something within her seemed to be shuddering, shrinking, shriveling together, losing all semblance of what had been. She felt as if it was her heart; but it was only her love.

"This is the way my Uncle Archibald went—in a gallop—you know." He spoke with a certain derision and in little gasps, as if breath were failing him. "There's no danger of that for me, of course, once I get south; but the doctors won't answer for me if I stay here during the coming fall and winter."

Then he held her in his arms with what seemed to be a frenzy of passion; a keen and quickened desire beside which his former and healthful transports were tempered and lukewarm by comparison.

"We need not wait, Dorothea," he whispered. "We must not put it off. Let the marriage be at once, and you will come with me and be with me. Oh, God! I feel as if

I would never let you go; as if I must hold you in my arms forever, night and day, and always!"

She attempted to withdraw from his embrace. She begged him not to think of it, and tried to convince him that it was impossible.

"I would only be a hindrance, Randall. You will come back well and strong; it will be time enough then," and to herself she was saying: "never, never, never!" There was a long silence, and he had closed his eyes again.

"For another reason, my Dorothea," and then he waited again, as one hesitates through shame or through fear, to speak. "I am quite—almost sure I shall get well; but the strongest of us cannot count upon life. If the worst should come I want you to have all I possess; what fortune I have must be yours, and marriage will make my wish secure. Now I'm getting morbid." He ended with a laugh that died away in a cough which threatened to wrench the breath from his body, and which brought the attendant, who had waited without, quickly to his side.

Dorothea watched him from the window descend the steps, leaning upon the man's arm, and saw him enter his carriage and fall helpless and exhausted as he had sunk an hour before in the corner of her sofa.

She was glad there was no one present to compel her to speak. She stayed at the window as if dazed, looking fixedly at the spot where the carriage had stood. A clock on the mantel striking the hour finally roused her, and she realized that there would soon be people appearing whom she would be forced to face and speak to.

Fifteen minutes later Dorothea had changed her house gown, had mounted her "wheel," and was fleeing as Death himself pursued her.

She sped along the familiar roadway, seemingly borne on by some force other than mechanical—some unwonted energy—a stubborn impulse that lighted her eyes, set her cheeks aflame, bent her supple body to one purpose—that was, swiftest flight.

How far, and how long did she go? She did not know, she did not care. The country about her grew unfamiliar. She was on a rough, unfrequented road, where the birds in the wayside bushes seemed unafraid. She could perceive no human habitation; an old fallow field, a stretch of wood, great trees bending thick-leaved branches, languidly, and flinging long, inviting shadows aslant the road; the weedy smell of summer; the drone of the insects, the sky and the clouds, and the quivering, lambent air. She was alone with nature; her pulses beating in unison with its sensuous throb, as she stopped and stretched herself upon the sward. Every muscle, nerve, fibre abandoned itself to the delicious sensation of rest that overtook and crept tingling through the whole length of her body.

She had never spoken a word after bidding him good bye; but now she seemed disposed to make confidants of

24

the tremulous leaves, or the crawling and hopping insects, or the big sky into which she was staring.

"Never!" she whispered, "not for all his thousands! Never, never! not for millions!"

The Godmother

I

Tante Elodie attracted youth in some incomprehensible way. It was seldom there was not a group of young people gathered about her fire in winter or sitting with her in summer, in the pleasant shade of the live-oaks that screened the gallery.

There were several persons forming a half circle around her generous chimney early one evening in February. There were Madame Nicolas's two tiny little girls who sat on the floor and played with a cat the whole time; Madame Nicolas herself, who only came for the little girls and insisted on hurrying away because it was time to put the children to bed, and who, moreover, was expecting a caller. There was a fair, blonde girl, one of the younger teachers at the Normal school. Gabriel Lucaze offered to escort her home when she got up to go, after Madame Nicolas's departure. But she had already accepted the company of a silent, studious looking youth who had come there in the hopes of meeting her. So they all went away but young Gabriel Lucaze, Tante Elodie's godson who stayed and played cribbage with her. They played a

a small table on which were a shaded lamp, a few magazines and a dish of *pralines* which the lady took great
pleasure in nibbling during the reflective pauses of the
game. They had played one game and were nearing the
end of the second. He laid a queen upon the table.

"Fifteen-two" she said, playing a five.

"Twenty, and a pair."

"Twenty-five. Six points for me."

"Its a 'go.' "

"Thirty-one and out. That is the second game I've won.
Will you play another rubber, Gabriel?"

"Not much, Tante Elodie, when you are playing in such
luck. Besides, I've got to get out, it's half-past-eight." He
had played recklessly, often glancing at the bronze clock
which reposed majestically beneath its crystal globe on
the mantlepiece. He prepared at once to leave, going before the gilt-framed, oval mirror to fold and arrange a silk
muffler beneath his great coat.

He was rather good looking. That is, he was healthy
looking; his face a little florid, and hair almost black. It
was short and curly and parted on one side. His eyes were
fine when they were not bloodshot, as they sometimes
were. His mouth might have been better. It was not dis-
agreeable or unpleasant, but it was unsatisfactory and
drooped a little at the corners. However, he was good to
look at as he crossed the muffler over his chest. His face
was unusually alert. Tante Elodie looked at him in the
glass.

"Will you be warm enough, my boy? It has turned ver cold since six o'clock."

"Plenty warm. Too warm."

"Where are you going?"

"Now, Tante Elodie," he said, turning, and laying hand on her shoulder; he was holding his soft felt hat i the other. "It is always 'where are you going?' 'Wher have you been?' I have spoiled you. I have told you to much. You expect me to tell you everything; consequentl I must sometimes tell you fibs. I am going to confessior There! are you satisfied?" and he bent down and gave he a hearty kiss.

"I am satisfied, provided you go to the right priestess confession; not up the hill, mind you!"

"Up the hill" meant up at the Normal school wit Tante Elodie. She was a very conservative person. "Th Normal" seemed to her an unpardonable innovation, wit its teachers from Minnesota, from Iowa, from God knows-where, bringing strange ways and manners to th old town. She was one, also, who considered the emanc pation of slaves a great mistake. She had many reason for thinking so and was often called upon to enumerat this in her wordy arguments with her many opponents.

II

Tante Elodie distinctly heard the Doctor leave the Widow
Nicolas's at a quarter past ten. He visited the handsome
and attractive young woman two evenings in the week
and always left at the same hour. Tante Elodie's double
glass doors opened upon the wide upper gallery. Around
the angle of the gallery were the apartments of Madame
Nicholas. Any one visiting the widow was obliged to pass
Tante Elodie's door. Beneath was a store occasionally occupied by some merchant or other, but oftener vacant. A
stairway led down from the porch to the yard where two
enormous live-oaks grew and cast a dense shade upon the
gallery above, making it an agreeable retreat and resting
place on hot summer afternoons. The high, wooden yard-
gate opened directly upon the street.

A half hour went by after the Doctor passed her door.
Tante Elodie played "solitaire." Another half hour followed and still Tante Elodie was not sleepy nor did she
think of going to bed. It was very near midnight when
she began to prepare her night toilet and to cover the fire.

The room was very large with heavy rafters across the
ceiling. There was an enormous bed over in the corner; a
four-posted mahogany covered with a lace spread which
was religiously folded every night and laid on a chair.
There were some old ambrotypes and photographs about

29

the room; a few comfortable but simple rocking chairs and a broad fire place in which a big log sizzled. It was an attractive room for anyone, not because of anything that was in it except Tante Elodie herself. She was far past fifty. Her hair was still soft and brown and her eyes bright and vivacious. Her figure was slender and nervous. There were many lines in her face, but it did not look care-worn. Had she her youthful flesh, she would have looked very young.

Tante Elodie had spent the evening in munching *pralines* and reading by lamp-light some old magazines that Gabriel Lucaze had brought her from the club.

There was a romance connected with her early days. Romances serve but to feed the imagination of the young; they add nothing to the sum of truth. No one realized this fact more strongly than Tante Elodie herself. While she tacitly condoned the romance, perhaps for the sake of the sympathy it bred, she never thought of Justin Lucaze but with a feeling of gratitude towards the memory of her parents who had prevented her marrying him thirty-five years before. She could have no connection between her deep and powerful affection for young Gabriel Lucaze and her old-time, brief passion for his father. She loved the boy above everything on earth. There was none so attractive to her as he; none so thoughtful of her pleasures and pains. In his devotion there was no trace of a duty-sense; it was the spontaneous expression of affection and seeming dependence.

30

After Tante Elodie had turned down her bed and undressed, she drew a gray flannel *peignoir* over her nightgown and knelt down to say her prayers; kneeling before a rocker with her bare feet turned to the fire. Prayers were no trifling matter with her. Besides those which she knew by heart, she read litanies and invocations from a book and also a chapter of "The Following of Christ." She had said her *Notre Père*, her *Salve Marie* and *Je crois en Dieu* and was deep in the litany of the Blessed Virgin when she fancied she heard footsteps on the stairs. The night was breathlessly still; it was very late.

"*Vierge des Vierges: Priez pour nous. Mère de Dieu: Priez—*"

Surely there was a stealthy step upon the gallery, and now a hand at her door, striving to lift the latch. Tante Elodie was not afraid. She felt the utmost security in her home and had no dread of mischievous intruders in the peaceful old town. She simply realized that there was some one at her door and that she must find out who it was and what they wanted. She got up from her knees, thrust her feet into her slippers that were near the fire and, lowering the lamp by which she had been reading her litanies, approached the door. There was the very softest rap upon the pane. Tante Elodie unbolted and opened the door the least bit.

"*Qui est là?*" she asked.

"Gabriel." He forced himself into the room before she had time to fully open the door to him.

III

Gabriel strode past her towards the fire, mechanically taking off his hat, and sat down in the rocker before which she had been kneeling. He sat on the prayer books she had left there. He removed them and laid them upon the table. Seeming to realize in a dazed way that it was not their accustomed place, he threw the two books on a nearby chair.

Tante Elodie raised the lamp and looked at him. His eyes were bloodshot, as they were when he drank or experienced any unusual emotion or excitement. But he was pale and his mouth drooped excessively, and twitched with the effort he made to control it. The top button was wrenched from his coat and his muffler was disarranged. Tante Elodie was grieved to the soul, seeing him thus. She thought he had been drinking.

"Gabriel, w'at is the matter?" she asked imploringly. "Oh, my poor child, w'at is the matter?" He looked at her in a fixed way and passed a hand over his head. He tried to speak, but his voice failed, as with one who experiences stage fright. Then he articulated, hoarsely, swallowing nervously between the slow words:

"I—killed a man—about an hour ago—yonder in the old Nigger-Luke Cabin." Tante Elodie's two hands were suddenly down to the table and she leaned heavily upon them for support.

"You did not; you did not," she panted. "You are drinking. You do not know w'at you are saying. Tell me, Gabriel, who 'as been making you drink? Ah! they will answer to me! You do not know w'at you are saying. *Boute!* how can you know!" She clutched him and the torn button that hung in the buttonhole fell to the floor.

"I don't know why it happened," he went on, gazing into the fire with unseeing eyes, or rather with eyes that saw what was pictured in his mind and not what was before them.

"I've been in cutting scrapes and shooting scrapes that never amounted to anything, when I was just as crazy mad as I was to-night. But I tell you, Tante Elodie, he's dead. I've got to get away. But how are you going to get out of a place like this, when every dog and cat"—His effort had spent itself, and he began to tremble with a nervous chill; his teeth chattered and his lips could not form an utterance.

Tante Elodie, stumbling rather than walking, went over to a small buffet and pouring some brandy into a glass, gave it to him. She took a little herself. She looked much older in the *peignoir* and the handkerchief tied around her head. She sat down beside Gabriel and took his hand. It was cold and clammy.

"Tell me everything," she said with determination, "everything; without delay; and do not speak so loud. We

33

shall see what must be done. Was it a negro? Tell me everything."

"No, it was a white man, you don't know, from Conshotta, named Everson. He was half drunk; a hulking bully as strong as an ox, or I could have licked him. He tortured me until I was frantic. Did you ever see a cat torment a mouse? The mouse can't do anything but lose its head. I lost my head, but I had my knife; that big hornhandled knife."

"Where is it?" she asked sharply. He felt his back pocket.

"I don't know." He did not seem to care, or to realize the importance of the loss.

"Go on; make haste; tell me the whole story. You went from here—you went—go on."

"I went down the river a piece," he said, throwing himself back in the chair and keeping his eyes fixed upon one burning ember on the hearth, "down to Symund's store where there was a game of cards. A lot of the fellows were there. I played a little and didn't drink anything, and stopped at ten. I was going"—He leaned forward with his elbows on his knees and his hands hanging between. "I was going to see a woman at eleven o'clock; it was the only time I could see her. I came along and when I got by the old Nigger-Luke Cabin I lit a match and looked at my watch. It was too early and it wouldn't do to hang around. I went into the cabin and started a blaze in the chimney with some fine wood I found there. My feet were

34

cold and I sat on an empty soap-box before the fire to dry them. I remember I kept looking at my watch. It was twenty-five minutes to eleven when Everson came into the cabin. He was half drunk and his face was red and looked like a beast. He had left the game and had followed me. I hadn't spoken of where I was going. But he said he knew I was off for a lark and he wanted to go along. I said he couldn't go where I was going, and there was no use talking. He kept it up. At a quarter to eleven I wanted to go, and he went and stood in the doorway.

" 'If I don't go, you don't go', he said, and he kept it up. When I tried to pass him he pushed me back like I was a feather. He didn't get mad. He laughed all the time and drank whiskey out of a bottle he had in his pocket. If I hadn't got mad and lost my head, I might have fooled him or played some trick on him—if I had used my wits. But I didn't know any more what I was doing than the day I threw the inkstand at old Dainean's head when he switched me and made fun of me before the whole school.

"I stooped by the fire and looked at my watch; he was talking all kinds of foolishness I can't repeat. It was eleven o'clock. I was in a killing rage and made a dash for the door. His big body and his big arm were there like an iron bar, and he laughed. I took out my knife and stuck it into him. I don't believe he knew at first that I had touched him, for he kept on laughing; then he fell over like a pig, and the old cabin shook."

Gabriel had raised his clinched hand with an intensely

dramatic movement when he said, "I stuck it into him."
Then he let his head fall back against the chair and fin
ished the concluding sentences of his story with close
eyes.

"How do you know he is dead?" asked Tante Elodi
whose voice sounded hard and monotonous.

"I only walked ten steps away and went back to see. H
was dead. Then I came here. The best thing is to go giv
myself up, I reckon, and tell the whole story like I've to
you. That's about the best thing I can do if I want an
peace of mind."

"Are you crazy, Gabriel! You have not yet regaine
your senses. Listen to me. Listen to me and try to unde
stand what I say."

Her face was full of a hard intelligence he had not see
there before; all the soft womanliness had for the momer
faded out of it.

"You 'ave not killed the man Everson," she said delil
erately. "You know nothing about 'im. You do not knov
that he left Symund's or that he followed you. You left a
ten o'clock. You came straight in town, not feeling wel
You saw a light in my window, came here; rapped on th
door; I let you in and gave you something for cramps i
the stomach and made you warm yourself and lie dow
on the sofa. Wait a moment. Stay still there."

She got up and went shuffling out the door, around th
angle of the gallery and tapped on Madame Nicolas

door. She could hear the young woman jump out of bed bewildered, asking, "Who is there? Wait! What is it?"

"It is Tante Elodie." The door was unbolted at once.

"Oh! how I hate to trouble you, *chérie*. Poor Gabriel 'as been at my room for hours with the most severe cramps. Nothing I can do seems to relieve 'im. Will you let me 'ave the morphine which Doctor left with you for old Besty's rheumatism? Ah! thank you. I think a quarter of a grain will relieve 'im. Poor boy! Such suffering! I am so sorry dear, to disturb you. Do not stand by the door, you will take cold. Good night."

Tante Elodie persuaded Gabriel, if the club were still open, to look in there on his way home. He had a room in a relative's house. His mother was dead and his father lived on a plantation several miles from town. Gabriel feared that his nerve would fail him. But Tante Elodie had him up again with a glass of brandy. She said that he must get the fact lodged in his mind that he was innocent. She inspected the young man carefully before he went away, brushing and arranging his toilet. She sewed the missing button on his coat. She had noticed some blood upon his right hand. He himself had not seen it. With a wet towel she washed his face and hands as though he were a little child. She brushed his hair and sent him away with a thousand reiterated precautions.

IV

Tante Elodie was not overcome in any way after Gabriel left her. She did not indulge in a hysterical moment, but set about accomplishing some purpose which she had evidently had in her mind. She dressed herself again; quickly, nervously, but with much precision. A shawl over her head and a long, black cape across her shoulders made her look like a nun. She quitted her room. It was very dark and very still out of doors. There was only a whispering wail among the live-oak leaves.

Tante Elodie stole noiselessly down the steps and out the gate. If she had met anyone, she intended to say she was suffering with toothache and was going to the doctor or druggist for relief.

But she met not a soul. She knew every plank, every uneven brick of the sidewalk; every rut of the way, and might have walked with her eyes closed. Strangely enough she had forgotten to pray. Prayer seemed to belong to her moments of contemplation; while now she was all action; prompt, quick, decisive action.

It must have been near upon two o'clock. She did not meet a cat or a dog on her way to the Nigger-Luke Cabin. The hut was well out of town and isolated from a group of tumbled-down shanties some distance off, in which a lazy set of negroes lived. There was not the slightest feeling of fear or horror in her breast. There might have been, had she not already been dominated and possessed by the determination that Gabriel must be shielded from ignominy—maybe, worse.

She glided into the low cabin like a shadow, hugging the side of the open door. She would have stumbled over the dead man's feet if she had not stepped so cautiously. The embers were burning so low that they gave but a faint glow in the sinister cabin with its obscure corners, its black, hanging cobwebs and the dead man lying twisted as he had fallen with his face on his arm.

Once in the cabin the woman crept towards the body on her hands and knees. She was looking for something in the dusky light; something she could not find. Crawling towards the fire over the uneven, creaking boards, she stirred the embers the least bit with a burnt stick that had fallen to one side. She dared not make a blaze. Then she dragged herself once more towards the lifeless body. She pictured how the knife had been thrust in; how it had fallen from Gabriel's hand; how the man had come down like a felled ox. Yes, the knife could not be far off, but she could not discover a trace of it. She slipped her fingers beneath the body and felt all along. The knife lay up under his arm pit. Her hand scraped his chin as she withdrew it. She did not mind. She was exultant at getting the knife. She felt like some other being, possessed by Satan. Some fiend in human shape, some spirit of murder. A cricket began to sing on the hearth.

Tante Elodie noticed the golden gleam of the murdered man's watch chain, and a sudden thought invaded her. With deft, though unsteady fingers, she unhooked the watch and chain. There was money in his pockets. She emptied them, turning the pockets inside out. It was difficult to reach his left hand pockets, but she did so. The money, a few bank notes and some silver coins, together with the watch and knife she tied in her handkerchief. Then she hurried away, taking a long stride across the man's body in order to reach the door.

The stars were like shining pieces of gold upon dark velvet. So Tante Elodie thought as she looked up at them an instant.

There was the sound of disorderly voices away off in the negro shanties. Clasping the parcel close to her breast she began to run. She ran, ran, as fast as some fleet fourfooted creature, ran, panting. She never stopped till she reached the gate that let her in under the live-oaks. The most intent listener could not have heard her as she mounted the stairs; as she let herself in at the door; as she bolted it. Once in the room she began to totter. She was sick to her stomach and her head swam. Instinctively she reached out towards the bed, and fell fainting upon it, face downward.

The gray light of dawn was coming in at her windows. The lamp on the table had burned out. Tante Elodie groaned as she tried to move. And again she groaned with mental anguish, this time as the events of the past night came back to her, one by one, in all their horrifying details. Her labor of love, begun the night before, was not yet ended. The parcel containing the watch and money were there beneath her, pressing into her bosom. When she managed to regain her feet the first thing which she did was to rekindle the fire with splinters of pine and pieces of hickory that were at hand in her wood box. When the fire was burning briskly, Tante Elodie took the paper money from the little bundle and burned it. She did not notice the denomination of the bills, there were five or six, she thrust them into the blaze with the poker and watched them burn. The few loose pieces of silver she put in her purse, apart from her own money; there was sixty-five cents in small coin. The watch she placed between her mattresses; then, seized with misgiving, took it out. She gazed around the room, seeing a safe hiding place and finally put the watch into a large, strong stocking which she pinned securely around her waist beneath her clothing. The knife she washed carefully, drying it with pieces of newspaper which she burned. The water in which she had washed it she also threw in a corner of the large fire place upon a heap of ashes. Then she put the knife into the pocket of one of Gabriel's coats which she had cleaned and mended for him; it was hanging in her closet.

She did all this slowly and with great effort, for she felt very sick. When the unpleasant work was over it was all she could do to undress and get beneath the covers of her bed.

She knew that when she did not appear at breakfast Madame Nicolas would send to investigate the cause of her absence. She took her meals with the young widow around the corner of the gallery. Tante Elodie was not rich. She received a small income from the remains of what had once been a magnificent plantation adjoining the lands which Justin Lucaze owned and cultivated. But she lived frugally, with a hundred small cares and economies and rarely felt the want of extra money except when the generosity of her nature prompted her to help an afflicted neighbor, or to bestow a gift upon some one of whom she was fond. It often seemed to Tante Elodie that all the affection of her heart was centered upon her young protégé, Gabriel; that what she felt for others was simply an emanation—rays, as it were, from this central sun of love that shone for him alone.

In the midst of twinges, of nervous tremors, her thoughts were with him. It was impossible for her to think of anything else. She was filled with unspeakable dread that he might betray himself. She wondered what he had done after he left her: what he was doing at that moment? She wanted to see him again alone, to insist anew upon the necessity of his self-assertion of innocence.

As she expected, Mrs. Wm. Nicholas came around at the breakfast hour to see what was the matter. She was an active woman, very pretty and fresh looking, with willing, deft hands and the kindest voice and eyes. She was distressed at the spectacle of poor Tante Elodie extended in bed with her head tied up, and looking pale and suffering.

"Ah! I suspected it!" she exclaimed, "coming out in the cold on the gallery last night to get morphine for Gabriel; *ma foi!* as if he could not go to the drug store for his morphine! Where have you pain? Have you any fever, Tante Elodie?"

"It is nothing, *chérie*. I believe I am only tired and want to rest for a day in bed."

"Then you must rest as long as you want. I will look after your fire and see that you have what you need. I will bring your coffee at once. It is a beautiful day; like spring. When the sun gets very warm I will open the window."

V

All day long Gabriel did not appear, and she dared not make inquiries about him. Several persons came in to see her, learning that she was sick. The midnight murder in the Nigger-Luke Cabin seemed to be the favorite subject of conversation among her visitors. They were not greatly excited over it as they might have been were the man other than a comparative stranger. But the subject seemed full of interest, enhanced by the mystery surrounding it. Madame Nicolas did not risk to speak of it.

"That is not a fit conversation for a sick-room. Any

doctor—anybody with sense will tell you. For Mercy's sake! change the subject."

But Fifine Delonce could not be silenced.

"And now it appears," she went on with renewed animation, "it appears he was playing cards down at Symund's store. That shows how they pass their time—those boys! It's a scandal! But nobody can remember when he left. Some say at nine, some say it was past eleven. He sort of went away like he didn't want them to notice."

"Well, we didn't know the man. My patience! there are murders every day. If we had to keep up with them, *ma foi!* Who is going to Lucie's card party tomorrow? I hear she did not invite her cousin Claire. They have fallen out again it seems." And Madame Nicolas, after speaking, went to give Tante Elodie a drink of *Tisane.*

"Mr. Ben's got about twenty darkies from Niggerville, holding them on suspicion," continued Fifine, dancing on the edge of her chair. "Without doubt the man was enticed to the cabin and murdered and robbed there. Not a picayune left in his pockets! only his pistol—that they didn't take, all loaded, in his back pocket, that he might have used, and his watch gone! Mr. Ben thinks his brother in Conshotta, that's very well off, is going to offer a big reward."

"What relation was the man to you, Fifine?" asked Madame Nicolas, sarcastically.

"He was a human being, Amelia; you have no heart, no

feeling. If it makes a woman that hard to associate with a doctor, then thank God—well—as I was saying, if they can catch those two strange section hands that left town last night—but you better bet they're not such fools to keep that watch. But old Uncle Marte said he saw little foot prints like a woman's early this morning, but no one wanted to listen to him or pay any attention, and the crowd tramped them out in little or no time. None of the boys want to let on; they don't want us to know which ones were playing cards at Symund's. Was Gabriel at Symund's, Tante Elodie?"

Tante Elodie coughed painfully and looked blankly as though she had only heard her name and had been inattentive to what was said.

"For pity sake leave Tante Elodie out of this! It's bad enough she has to listen, suffering as she is. Gabriel spent the evening here, on Tante Elodie's sofa, very sick with cramps. You will have to pursue your detective work in some other quarter, my dear."

A little girl came in with a huge bunch of blossoms. There was some bustle attending the arrangement of the flowers in vases, and in the midst of it, two or three ladies took their leave.

"I wonder if they're going to send the body off to-night, or if they're going to keep it for the morning train," Fifine was heard to speculate, before the door closed upon her.

Tante Elodie could not sleep that night. The following day she had some fever and Madame Nicolas insisted upon her seeing the doctor. He gave her a sleeping draught and some fever drops and said she would be all right in a few days; for he could find nothing alarming in her condition.

By a supreme effort of the will she got up on the third day hoping in the accustomed routine of her daily life to get rid, in part, of the uneasiness and unhappiness that possessed her.

The sun shone warm in the afternoon and she went and stood on the gallery watching for Gabriel to pass. He had not been near her. She was wounded, alarmed, miserable at his silence and absence; but determined to see him. He came down the street, presently, never looking up, with his hat drawn over his eyes.

"Gabriel!" she called. He gave a start and glanced around.

"Come up; I want to see you a moment."

"I haven't time now, Tante Elodie."

"Come in!" she said sharply.

"All right, you'll have to fix it up with Morrison," and he opened the gate and went in. She was back in her room by the time he reached it, and in her chair, trembling a little and feeling sick again.

"Gabriel, if you 'ave no heart, it seems to me you would 'ave some intelligence; a moment's reflection would show you the folly of altering your 'abits so suddenly. Did you not know I was sick? Did you not guess my uneasiness?"

"I haven't guessed anything or known anything but a taste of hell," he said, not looking at her. Her heart bled afresh for him and went out to him in full forgiveness. "You were right," he went on, "it would have been horrible to say anything. There is no suspicion. I'll never say anything unless someone should be falsely accused."

"There will be no possible evidence to accuse anyone," she assured him. "Forget it, forget it. Keep on as though it was something you had dreamed. Not only for the outside, but within yourself. Do not accuse yourself of that act, but the actions, the conduct, the ungovernable temper that made it possible. Promise me it will be a lesson to you, Gabriel; and God, who reads men's hearts, will not call it a crime, but an accident which your unbridled nature invited. I will forget it. You must forget it. 'Ave you been to the office?"

"Today; not yesterday. I don't know what I did yesterday, but look for the knife—after they—I couldn't go while he was there—and I thought every minute some one was coming to accuse me. And when I realized they weren't—I don't know—I drank too much, I think. Reading law! I might as well have been reading Hebrew. If Morrison thinks—See here Tante Elodie, are there any spots on this coat? Can you see anything here in the light?"

"There are no spots anywhere. Stop thinking of it, I implore you." But he pulled off the coat and flung it across a chair. He went to the closet to get his other coat which

47

he knew hung there. Tante Elodie, still feeble and suffering, in the depths of her chair, was not quick enough, could think of no way to prevent it. She had at first put the knife in his pocket with the intention of returning it to him. But now she dreaded to have him find it, and thus discover the part she had played in the sickening dream.

He buttoned up his coat briskly and started away.

"Please burn it," he said, looking at the garment on the chair. "I never want to see it again."

VI

When it became distinctly evident that no slightest suspicion would be attached to him for the killing of Everson; when he plainly realized that there was no one upon whom the guilt could be fastened, Gabriel thought he would regain his lost equilibrium. If in no other way, he fancied he could reason himself back into it. He was suffering, but he someway had no fear that his present condition of mind would last. He thought it would pass away like a malignant fever. It would have to pass away or it would have to kill him.

From Tante Elodie's he went over to Morrison's office where he was reading law. Morrison and his partner were out of town and he had the office to himself. He had been there all morning. There was nothing for him to do now but to see anyone who called on business, and to go or with his reading. He seated himself and spread his book before him, but he looked into the street through the open door. Then he got up and shut the door. He again fastened his eyes upon the pages before him, but his mind was traveling other ways. For the hundredth time he was going over every detail of the fatal night, and trying to justify himself in his own heart.

If it had been an open and fair fight there would have been no trouble in squaring himself with his conscience; if the man had shown the slightest disposition to do him bodily harm, but he had not. On the other hand, he asked himself, what constituted a murder? Why, there was Morrison himself who had once fired at Judge Filips on that very street. His ball had gone wide of the mark, and subsequently he and Filips had adjusted their difficulties and become friends. Was Morrison any less a murderer because his weapon had missed?

Suppose the knife had swerved, had penetrated the arm, had inflicted a harmless scratch or flesh wound, would he be sitting there now, calling himself names? But he would try to think it all out later. He could not bear to be there alone, he never liked to be alone, and now he could not endure it. He closed the book without the slightest recollection of a line his eyes had followed. He went and gazed up and down the street, then he locked the office and walked away.

The fact of Everson having been robbed was very puzzling to Gabriel. He thought about it as he walked along the street.

The complete change that had taken place in his emotions, his sentiments, did not astonish him in the least: we accept such phenomena without question. A week ago—not so long as that—he was in love with the fair-haired girl up at the Normal. He was undeniably in love with her. He knew the symptoms. He wanted to marry her and meant to ask her whenever his position justified him in doing so.

Now, where had that love gone? He thought of her with indifference. Still, he was seeking her at that moment, through habit, without any special motive. He had no positive desire to see her; to see any one; and yet he could not endure to be alone. He had no desire to see Tante Elodie. She wanted him to forget and her presence made him remember.

The girl was walking under the beautiful trees, and she stood and waited for him, when she saw him mounting the hill. As he looked at her, his fondness for her and his intentions toward her, appeared now, like child's play. Life was something terrible of which she had no conception. She seemed to him as harmless, as innocent, as insignificant as a little bird.

"Oh! Gabriel," she exclaimed. "I had just written you a note. Why haven't you been here? It was foolish to get offended. I wanted to explain: I couldn't get out of it the other night, at Tante Elodie's, when he asked me. You know I couldn't, and that I would rather have come with you." Was it possible he would have taken this seriously a week ago?

"Delonce is a good fellow; he's a decent fellow. I don't blame you. That's all right." She was hurt at his easy complaisance. She did not wish to offend him, and here she was grieved because he was not offended.

"Will you come indoors to the fire?" she asked.

"No; I just strolled up for a minute." He leaned against a tree and looked bored, or rather, preoccupied with other things than herself. It was not a week ago that he wanted to see her every day; when he said the hours were like minutes that he passed beside her. "I just strolled up to tell you that I am going away."

"Oh! going away?" and the pink deepened in her cheeks, and she tried to look indifferent and to clasp her glove tighter. He had not the slightest intention of going away when he mounted the hill. It came to him like an inspiration.

"Where are you going?"

"Going to look for work in the city."

"And what about your law studies?"

"I have no talent for the law; it's about time I acknowledged it. I want to get into something that will make me hustle. I wouldn't mind—I'd like to get something to do on a railroad that would go tearing through the country night and day. What's the matter?" he asked, perceiving the tears that she could not conceal.

"Nothing's the matter," she answered with dignity, and a sense of seeming proud.

He took her word for it and, instead of seeking to console her, went rambling on about the various occupations in which he should like to engage for a while.

"When are you going?"

"Just as soon as I can."

"Shall I see you again?"

"Of course. Good-bye. Don't stay out here too long; you might take cold." He listlessly shook hands with her and descended the hill with long rapid strides.

He would not intentionally have hurt her. He did not realize that he was wounding her. It would have been as difficult for him to revive his passion for her as to bring Everson back to life. Gabriel knew there could be fresh horror added to the situation. Discovery would have added to it; a false accusation would have deepened it. But he never dreamed of the new horror coming as it did, through Tante Elodie, when he found the knife in his pocket. It took a long time to realize what it meant; and then he felt as if he never wanted to see her again. In his mind, her action identified itself with his crime, and made itself a hateful, hideous part of it, which he could not endure to think of, and of which he could not help thinking.

It was the one thing which had saved him, and yet he felt no gratitude. The great love which had prompted the deed did not soften him. He could not believe that any man was worth loving to such length, or worth saving at such a price. She seemed, to his imagination, less a woman than a monster, capable of committing, in cold-blood, deeds, which he himself could only accomplish in blind rage. For the first time, Gabriel wept. He threw himself down upon the ground in the deepening twilight and wept as he never had before in his life. A terrible sense of loss overpowered him; as if someone dearer than a mother had been taken out of the reach of his heart; as if a refuge had gone from him. The last spark of human affection was dead within him. He knew it as he was losing it. He wept at the loss which left him alone with his thoughts.

VII

Tante Elodie was always chilly. It was warm for the last of April, and the women at Madame Nicolas's wedding were all in airy summer attire. All but Tante Elodie, who wore her black silk, her old silk with a white lace fichu, and she held an embroidered handkerchief and a fan in her hand.

Fifine Delonce had been over in the morning to take up the seams in the dress, for, as she expressed herself, it was miles too loose for Tante Elodie's figure. She appeared to be shrivelling away to nothing. She had not again been sick in bed since that little spell in February; but she was plainly wasting and was very feeble. Her eyes, though, were as bright as ever; sometimes they looked as hard as

53

flint. The doctor, whom Madame Nicolas insisted upon her seeing occasionally, gave a name to her disease; it was a Greek name and sounded convincing. She was taking a tonic especially prepared for her, from a large bottle, three times a day.

Fifine was a great gossip. When and how she gathered her news nobody could tell. It was always said she knew ten times more than the weekly paper would dare to print. She often visited Tante Elodie, and she told her news of everyone; among others of Gabriel.

It was she who told that he had abandoned the study of the law. She told Tante Elodie when he started for the city to look for work and when he came back from the fruitless search.

"Did you know that Gabriel is working on the railroad, now? Fireman! Think of it! What a comedown from reading law in Morrison's office. If I were a man, I'd try to have more strength of character than to go to the dogs on account of a girl; an insignificant somebody from Kansas! Even if she is going to marry my brother, I must say it was no way to treat a boy—leading him on, especially a boy like Gabriel, that any girl would have been glad—Well, it's none of my business; only I'm sorry he took it like he did. Drinking himself to death, they say."

That morning, as she was taking up the seams of the silk dress, there was fresh news of Gabriel. He was tired of the railroad, it seemed. He was down on his father's place herding cattle, breaking in colts, drinking like a fish.

"I wouldn't have such a thing on my conscience! Goodness me! I couldn't sleep at nights if I was that girl."

Tante Elodie always listened with a sad, resigned smile. It did not seem to make any difference whether she had Gabriel or not. He had broken her heart and he was killing her. It was not his crime that had broken her heart; it was his indifference to her love and his turning away from her.

It was whispered about that Tante Elodie had grown indifferent to her religion. There was no truth in it. She had not been to confession for two months; but otherwise she followed closely the demands made upon her, redoubling her zeal in church work and attending mass each morning.

At the wedding she was holding quite a little reception of her own in the corner of the gallery. The air was mild and pleasant. Young people flocked about her and occasionally the radiant bride came out to see if she were comfortable and if there was anything she wanted to eat or drink.

A young girl leaning over the railing suddenly exclaimed "*Tiens!* someone is dead. I didn't know any one was sick." She was watching the approach of a man who was coming down the street, distributing, according to the custom of the country, a death notice from door to door.

He wore a long black coat and walked with a measured tread. He was as expressionless as an automaton; handing the little slips of paper at every door; not missing one. The girl, leaning over the railing, went to the head of the stairs to receive the notice when he entered Tante Elodie's gate.

The small, single sheet, which he gave her, was bordered in black and decorated with an old-fashioned wood cut of a weeping willow beside a grave. It was an announcement on the part of Monsieur Justin Lucaze of the death of his only son, Gabriel, who had been instantly killed, the night before, by a fall from his horse.

If the automaton had had any sense of decency, he might have skipped the house of joy, in which there was a wedding feast, in which there was the sound of laughter, the click of glasses, the hum of merry voices, and a vision of sweet women with their thoughts upon love and marriage and earthly bliss. But he had no sense of decency. He was as indifferent and relentless as Death, whose messenger he was.

The sad news, passed from lip to lip, cast a shadow as if a cloud had flitted across the sky. Tante Elodie alone stayed in its shadow. She sank deeper down into the rocker, more shrivelled than ever. They all remembered Tante Elodie's romance and respected her grief.

She did not speak any more, or even smile, but wiped her forehead with the old lace handkerchief and sometimes closed her eyes. When she closed her eyes she pictured Gabriel dead, down there on the plantation, with his father watching beside him. He might have betrayed himself had he lived. There was nothing now to betray him. Even the shining gold watch lay deep in a gorged ravine where she had flung it when she once walked through the country alone at dusk.

She thought of her own place down there beside Justin's, all dismantled, with bats beating about the eaves and negroes living under the falling roof.

Tante Elodie did not seem to want to go in doors again. The bride and groom went away. The guests went away, one by one, and all the little children. She stayed there alone in the corner, under the deep shadows of the oaks while the stars came out to keep her company.

PENGUIN 60s CLASSICS

APOLLONIUS OF RHODES · *Jason and the Argonauts*
ARISTOPHANES · *Lysistrata*
SAINT AUGUSTINE · *Confessions of a Sinner*
JANE AUSTEN · *The History of England*
HONORÉ DE BALZAC · *The Atheist's Mass*
BASHŌ · *Haiku*
GIOVANNI BOCCACCIO · *Ten Tales from the* Decameron
JAMES BOSWELL · *Meeting Dr Johnson*
CHARLOTTE BRONTË · *Mina Laury*
CAO XUEQIN · *The Dream of the Red Chamber*
THOMAS CARLYLE · *On Great Men*
BALDESAR CASTIGLIONE · *Etiquette for Renaissance Gentlemen*
CERVANTES · *The Jealous Extremaduran*
KATE CHOPIN · *The Kiss*
JOSEPH CONRAD · *The Secret Sharer*
DANTE · *The First Three Circles of Hell*
CHARLES DARWIN · *The Galapagos Islands*
THOMAS DE QUINCEY · *The Pleasures and Pains of Opium*
DANIEL DEFOE · *A Visitation of the Plague*
BERNAL DÍAZ · *The Betrayal of Montezuma*
FYODOR DOSTOYEVSKY · *The Gentle Spirit*
FREDERICK DOUGLASS · *The Education of Frederick Douglass*
GEORGE ELIOT · *The Lifted Veil*
GUSTAVE FLAUBERT · *A Simple Heart*
BENJAMIN FRANKLIN · *The Means and Manner of Obtaining Virtue*
EDWARD GIBBON · *Reflections on the Fall of Rome*
CHARLOTTE PERKINS GILMAN · *The Yellow Wallpaper*
GOETHE · *Letters from Italy*
HOMER · *The Rage of Achilles*
HOMER · *The Voyages of Odysseus*

PENGUIN 60s CLASSICS

HENRY JAMES · *The Lesson of the Master*
FRANZ KAFKA · *The Judgement*
THOMAS À KEMPIS · *Counsels on the Spiritual Life*
HEINRICH VON KLEIST · *The Marquise of O—*
LIVY · *Hannibal's Crossing of the Alps*
NICCOLÒ MACHIAVELLI · *The Art of War*
SIR THOMAS MALORY · *The Death of King Arthur*
GUY DE MAUPASSANT · *Boule de Suif*
FRIEDRICH NIETZSCHE · *Zarathustra's Discourses*
OVID · *Orpheus in the Underworld*
PLATO · *Phaedrus*
EDGAR ALLAN POE · *The Murders in the Rue Morgue*
ARTHUR RIMBAUD · *A Season in Hell*
JEAN-JACQUES ROUSSEAU · *Meditations of a Solitary Walker*
ROBERT LOUIS STEVENSON · *Dr Jekyll and Mr Hyde*
TACITUS · *Nero and the Burning of Rome*
HENRY DAVID THOREAU · *Civil Disobedience*
LEO TOLSTOY · *The Death of Ivan Ilyich*
IVAN TURGENEV · *Three Sketches from a Hunter's Album*
MARK TWAIN · *The Man That Corrupted Hadleyburg*
GIORGIO VASARI · *Lives of Three Renaissance Artists*
EDITH WHARTON · *Souls Belated*
WALT WHITMAN · *Song of Myself*
OSCAR WILDE · *The Portrait of Mr W. H.*

ANONYMOUS WORKS

Beowulf and Grendel   *Buddha's Teachings*
Gilgamesh and Enkidu   *Krishna's Dialogue on the Soul*
Tales of Cú Chulaind   *Two Viking Romances*